THE
MOUNTAIN

THE
MOUNTAIN

Written
by
Judith Weinshall Liberman

Illustrated by Gail Davis

First published by Dog Ear Publishing
4010 W. 86th Street, Ste H
Indianapolis, IN 46268
www.dogearpublishing.net

ISBN: 978-1-4575-3134-7

Library of Congress Control Number: has been applied for

This book is printed on acid-free paper.

This book is a work of fiction. Places, events, and situations in this book are purely fictional and any resemblance to actual persons, living or dead, is coincidental.

Printed in the United States of America

****

This book is dedicated to
the author's dear grandson
DANIEL PERLMAN
whose likeness was used for the hero
****

Did you ever climb a mountain,
aiming for its peak?

Did you ever reach the top,
and live of it to speak?

I still recall the days when I
was a member of the Scouts.

We had to climb a mountain fraught
with dangers all about.

The mountain's peak was very high,
the dirt road was quite steep,

and often while I climbed and climbed,
I wished to stop and weep.

I met with snakes that hissed at me,
and bushes that me scratched.

The sun was hot and made me thirst.
Mates' speed could not be matched.

My shoes were tight, and right in back,
they chafed my skin, and so,

although I wore thick socks, my blood
would freely through them flow.

And all my mates were far ahead,
much closer to the top,

and as I watched them from afar,
I felt just like a flop.

So many times I thought I should
just quit and head straight down,

and go right back to rest my feet
in my cool home in town.

And yet I kept walking right on
for reasons I don't know,

and in due course I reached the peak,
where with great pride I'd glow.

And even though when I arrived
at that high mountain top,

my mates were on their way back down
and for me did not stop,

I did not care what others did,
nor what they might opine.

I felt great pride that I had reached
a goal that was now mine.

ALSO BY THE AUTHOR

INTRODUCTION TO PUBLIC INTERNATIONAL LAW (1955)

THE BIRD'S LAST SONG (Illustrated by the author) (1976)

HOLOCAUST WALL HANGINGS (2002)

MY LIFE INTO ART: An Autobiography (2007)

LOOKING BACK: Four Plays (2010)

ON BEING AN ARTIST: Three Plays and a Libretto (2012)

REFLECTIONS: Poems, Lyrics, and Stories (With Laura Liberman, M.D.) (2012)

ICE CREAM SNOW (Illustrated by the author) (2012)

PASSION: Poems of Love and Protest (2013)

ZINA: A Selection from Her Poems and Photographs (2013)

THE LITTLE FAIRY (Illustrated by Gail Davis) (2013)

COLOR IN OUR WORLD (Illustrated by the author with photographs) (2014)

THE VERY OLD PAINTER AND HER HUSBAND (Illustrated by Gail Davis) (2014)

HAIFA: My Home Town (Illustrated by Radu Costea) (2014)

ANGEL'S PUPPIES (Illustrated by Gail Davis) (2014)

THE GIANT HOUSE (Illustrated by Gail Davis) (2014)

THE BEE AND THE BUTTERFLY (Illustrated by Radu Costea) (2014)

CPSIA information can be obtained
at www.ICGtesting.com
Printed in the USA
BVIC01n1832210914
367670BV00001B/1